EASY READERS

A Beginning-to-Read Book

Little Red Riding Hood

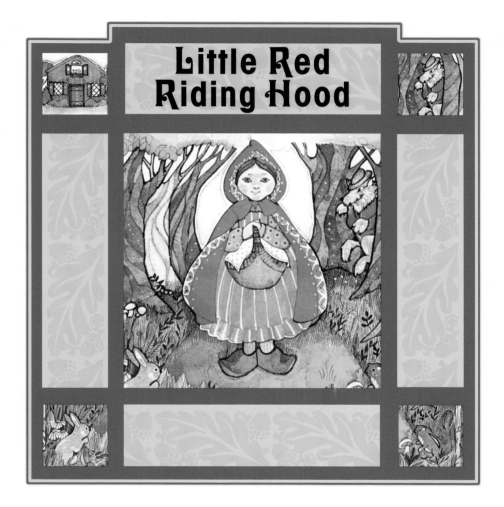

by Margaret Hillert

Illustrated by Gwen Connelly

NORWOOD HOUSE PRESS

DEAR CAREGIVER, The *Beginning-to-Read* series is a carefully written collection of classic readers you may remember from your own childhood. Each book features text comprised of common sight words to provide your child ample practice reading the words that appear most frequently in written text. The many additional details in the pictures enhance the story and offer the opportunity for you to help your child expand oral language and develop comprehension.

Begin by reading the story to your child, followed by letting him or her read familiar words and soon your child will be able to read the story independently. At each step of the way, be sure to praise your reader's efforts to build his or her confidence as an independent reader. Discuss the pictures and encourage your child to make connections between the story and his or her own life. At the end of the story, you will find reading activities and a word list that will help your child practice and strengthen beginning reading skills.

Above all, the most important part of the reading experience is to have fun and enjoy it!

Shannon Cannon

Shannon Cannon,
Literacy Consultant

Norwood House Press • P.O. Box 316598 • Chicago, Illinois 60631
For more information about Norwood House Press please visit our website at *www.norwoodhousepress.com* or call 866-565-2900.

LIBRARY OF CONGRESS CATALOGING-IN-PUBLICATION DATA

Hillert, Margaret.
  Little Red Riding Hood / by Margaret Hillert ; illustrated by Gwen Connelly.— Rev. and expanded library ed.
    p. cm. — (Beginning to read. Fairy tales and folklore)
  Summary: A little girl meets a wolf in the forest on her way to visit her grandmother. Includes reading activities.
  ISBN-13: 978-1-59953-022-2 (library edition : alk. paper)
  ISBN-10: 1-59953-022-8 (library edition : alk. paper)
  [1. Fairy tales. 2. Folklore. 3. Readers.] I. Connelly, Gwen, ill. II. Little Red Riding Hood. English. III. Title. IV. Series.
  PZ8.H5425Li 2006
  398.2—dc22   2005033496

Beginning-to-Read series © 2006 by Margaret Hillert.
Library edition published by permission of Pearson Education, Inc. in arrangement with Norwood House Publishing Company. All rights reserved. This book was originally published by Follett Publishing Company in 1982.

Mother said, "Look here, little one.
Here is something for you.
Something red.
See how it looks on you."

4

The little girl said, "Oh, Mother.
How pretty it is!
I like it.
I like red."

"Now," said Mother,
"I want you to do something.
I want you to go to
Grandmother's house."

"Oh, good," said the girl.
"I like to do that.
  It is fun."

"Yes," said Mother.
"And here is something good
   to eat.
   Take it to Grandmother.
   Go on, now.
   Do not play on the way."

"No, Mother," said the girl.
"I will not play.
I will run, run, run."

Oh, I like it here.
This is fun.
And I see something pretty.
Something pretty for Grandmother.

Red ones.
Yellow ones.
Blue ones.
I will get this and this
and this.

Oh, what do I see now?
Something big, big, big.
Do I like this big one?

"Yes. I am big,
but I like you.
I will walk with you.
What do you have?"

"I have something pretty
for my grandmother.
And I have something good
to eat."

"That is good.
You are a good girl,
but I have to go now.
I have to run."

And I have to run, too.
Where is Grandmother's house?
Oh, I see it.
That is it.

"Grandmother, Grandmother.
Here I am.
I have come to see you.
I have something for you."

"Come in. Come in.
Come here to me.
I want a good
look at you."

"Oh, how did you get in here?
You look like Grandmother,
but you are not Grandmother.
Where is Grandmother?
Did you eat my grandmother?
I do not like you.
Help, help!"

"Here I come," said a man.
"I will help you.
See what I can do.
I can make this big one
run away."

"Get out. Get out,"
said the man.
"Go away.
We do not want you here."

"But where is Grandmother?
I do not see Grandmother.
Oh, I want my grandmother."

"Here I am, little one," said Grandmother.
"He did not eat me.
Come here to me.
My, how good it is to see you!"

The following activities support the findings of the National Reading Panel that determined the most effective components for reading instruction are: Phonemic Awareness, Phonics, Vocabulary, Fluency, and Text Comprehension.

Phonemic Awareness: The /l/ sound

Substitution: Say the following words to your child and ask him or her to substitute the first sound in the word with /l/:

race = lace	cake = lake	pot = lot	dove = love
bean = lean	sick = lick	mist = list	jump = lump
cook = look	night = light		

Phonics: The letter L l

1. Demonstrate how to form the letters **L** and **l** for your child.

2. Have your child practice writing **L** and **l** at least three times each.

3. Ask your child to point to the words in the book that start with the letter **l**.

4. Write down the following words and ask your child to circle the letter **l** in each word:

girl	look	walk	will	little	yellow
mail	like	lunch	film	land	wolf
leaf	peel	talent	fall	left	pile

Vocabulary: Compound Words

1. Explain to your child that sometimes two words can be put together to make a new word. These are called compound words. The story has two compound words: *something*, and *grandmother*.

2. Write down the following words on separate pieces of paper:

bird	stick	back	boat	fire	house
light	row	bend	sail	yard	day
book	note	place	wood	candle	pack

3. Help your child move the pieces of paper around to form compound words.

   Possible answers: birdhouse, firehouse, fireplace, firewood, fireboat, houseboat, rowboat, sailboat, yardstick, candlestick, backyard, backbend, backpack, daylight, notebook

Fluency: Reader's Theater

1. Reread the story to your child at least two more times while your child tracks the print by running a finger under the words as they are read. Ask your child to read the words he or she knows with you.

2. Decide who will be Little Red Riding Hood, and who will be the other characters. Reread the story with each reader reading only his or her own part(s).

3. Practice reading with expression and changing voices for the characters.

Text Comprehension: Discussion Time

1. Ask your child to retell the sequence of events in the story.

2. To check comprehension, ask your child the following questions:

   • How did Little Red Riding Hood get her name?

   • What did Little Red Riding Hood stop and do on the way to her grandmother's house?

   • How did Little Red Riding Hood feel after the man chased away the wolf? How do you know?

   • Describe a time when you were scared? Who helped you feel better and how?

WORD LIST

Little Red Riding Hood uses the 69 words listed below.
This list can be used to practice reading the words that appear in the text.
You may wish to write the words on index cards and use them to help your
child build automatic word recognition. Regular practice with these words
will enhance your child's fluency in reading connected text.

a	for	I	oh	this
am	fun	in	on	to
and		is	one (s)	too
are	get	it	out	
at	girl			walk
away	go	like	play	want
	good	little	pretty	way
big	grandmother (s)	look (s)		what
blue			red	where
but	have	make	run	will
	he	man		with
can	help	me	said	
come	here	Mother	see	yellow
	house	my	something	yes
did	how			you
do		no	take	
		not	that	
eat		now	the	

ABOUT THE AUTHOR Margaret Hillert has written over 80 books for
children who are just learning to read. Her books
have been translated into many different languages and over a million children
throughout the world have read her books. She first started writing poetry as
a child and has continued to write for children and adults throughout her life. A
first grade teacher for 34 years, Margaret is now retired from teaching and lives in
Michigan where she likes to write, take walks in the morning, and care for her three cats.

Photograph by Glenna Washburn

ABOUT THE ADVISER Shannon Cannon contributed the activities pages that appear in
this book. Shannon serves as a literacy consultant and provides
staff development to help improve reading instruction. She is a frequent presenter at educational
conferences and workshops. Prior to this she worked as an elementary school teacher and as
president of a curriculum publishing company.